Written by Paul Shipton
Illustrated by Nadine Wickenden

Where's his hat?
Can you see it?

No!

Where's his coat?
Can you see it?

No!

Where's his scarf?
Can you see it?

No!

Where are his boots? Can you see them?

No!

Where is he?
Can you see him?

Yes!

The gallery

Ideas for reading

Written by Clare Dowdall BA(Ed), MA(Ed)
Lecturer and Primary Literacy Consultant

Learning objectives: read a range of familiar and common words and simple sentences independently; show an understanding of the elements of stories, such as main character, sequence of events, and openings; retell narratives in the correct sequence, drawing on the language patterns of stories; extend their vocabulary, exploring the meaning and sounds of new words; use language to imagine and recreate roles and experiences

Curriculum links: Creative Development: Responding to experiences; Expressing and communicating ideas

High frequency words: at, the, can, you, see, it, no, are, he, yes

Interest words: night, gallery, where's, hat, coat, scarf, boots

Resources: paper and pencils

Word count: 41

Getting started

- Ask children where portraits are hung. Introduce the word *gallery* and describe what this is for children who have not visited one.
- Explain that the book is about a gallery where strange things happen to the people in the portraits in the night.
- Look at the front and back covers together. Read the title and blurb together, pointing to each word with your finger and encouraging the children to join in.
- Ensure children understand the difference between a speech bubble and a thought bubble.

Reading and responding

- Turn to pp2–3. Read aloud with the children, pointing to each word as you read. Check that children understand who the characters are and what they are looking for.
- Ask children to look carefully at the pictures on p3 to find the man's hat. Encourage them to suggest what has happened to it, e.g. *He has given it to the lady in the next picture.*